This book belongs to:

_____

_____

_____

First published by Walker Books Ltd.
87 Vauxhall Walk, London SE11 5HJ

Copyright © 2002 by Lucy Cousins
Lucy Cousins font copyright © 2002 by Lucy Cousins

Based on the Audio Visual Series "Maisy" A King Rollo Films Production for
Universal Pictures Visual Programming. Original Script by Jeanne Willis.

Maisy™. Maisy is a registered trademark of Walker Books Ltd., London.

First U.S. paperback edition 2000

Library of Congress Cataloging-in-Publication Data
Cousins, Lucy.
Maisy takes a bath / Lucy Cousins.—1st ed.
p.   cm.
Summary: When Tallulah comes to visit twice at bathtime
she finally decides to join Maisy in the bath to play.
ISBN 0-7636-1082-8 (hardcover) — ISBN 0-7636-1084-4 (paperback)
[1. Baths—Fiction. 2. Play—Fiction. 3. Mice—Fiction.] I. Title.
PZ7.C83175 Mait 2000
[E]—dc21   99-053240

10

Printed in China

This book was typeset in Lucy Cousins.
The illustrations were done in gouache.

Candlewick Press
2067 Massachusetts Avenue
Cambridge, Massachusetts 02140

visit us at www.candlewick.com

Maisy Takes a Bath

Lucy Cousins

CANDLEWICK PRESS
CAMBRIDGE, MASSACHUSETTS

It's Maisy's bathtime.

She runs the water and puts in some bubbles...

and in goes Duck.

Ding, Dong!
Oh, that's
the doorbell.

Maisy runs downstairs to see who it is.

Hello, Tallulah.

Maisy can't play now. It's her bathtime.

Maisy runs back upstairs and gets undressed.

Maisy jumps into the bubbly bath.

Ding, Dong!
Who is ringing the doorbell now?

Hello again, Tallulah!

Maisy is still taking her bath. Come and play later.

Oh! Where are you going, Tallulah?

Tallulah runs up
to the bathroom
and takes off
her clothes.

Splash, splash!

Maisy and Tallulah
play in the bath.

Hooray!

Lucy Cousins is one of today's most acclaimed author-illustrators of children's books. Her unique titles instantly engage babies, toddlers, and preschoolers with their childlike simplicity and bright colors. And the winsome exploits of characters like Maisy reflect the adventures that young children have every day.

Lucy admits that illustration comes more easily to her than writing, which tends to work around the drawings. "I draw by heart," she says. "I think of what children would like by going back to my own childlike instincts." And what instincts! Lucy Cousins now has more than thirteen million books in print, from cloth and picture books to irresistible pull-the-tab and lift-the-flap books.